All inquiries should be addressed to:
Barron's Educational Series, Inc.
250 Wireless Boulevard
Hauppauge, New York 11788
www.barronseduc.com

ISBN: 978-0-7641-6749-2

Library of Congress Catalog Card No. 2014936262

Product conforms to all applicable CPSC and
CPSIA 2008 standards.
No lead or phthalate hazard.

Manufactured by M03I03D, Guangdong, China
Date of Manufacture: January 2015
9 8 7 6 5 4 3 2

Henry Is a Big Brother

by

Alyssa Satin Capucilli

Illustrations by Dorothy Stott

Hello! My name is Henry.
Today is a very special day.

Our new baby is coming home.
I'm a big brother! Hooray!

Mom told me stories of when I was a baby,
Dad showed me lots of pictures, too!

I wonder if our baby will have a smile just like mine?

What fun things will our baby like to do?

I hop, I skip, I wait and wait...

Our baby is home at last!

"Are you ready to meet your big brother, Henry?"
Mom and Dad very softly ask.

I climb on the couch all by myself;
Teddy sits with me.

Mom puts baby Casey gently in my lap...
Casey's tiny as can be!

We count the baby's fingers and toes,
"I did it!" I say with a cheer.

Then we find the baby's belly, eyes, and nose,

and even Casey's very little ears!

"Casey is too small to build with blocks,
and too small to swing and slide with me...
When will Casey be ready to play?
When will Casey be as big as me?"

"It took time for our family to grow," says Dad.
"It will take time for the baby to grow, too."
"Be patient Henry," promises Mom,
"There's lots of things a big brother can do!"

"Let's show Casey the cozy little crib!"
"Ta-da!" I lead the way!

I find Casey's rattle, and special blanket, too.
"Welcome to our room!" I say.

Waa-aa! Teddy holds his ears!

Casey starts to cry!

Is Casey getting hungry?

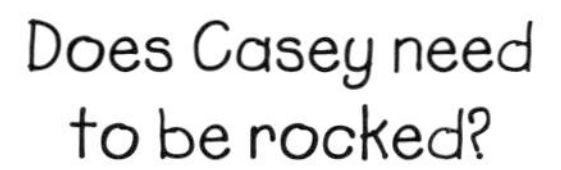

Does Casey need
to be rocked?

Or a diaper that is clean and dry?

I remember when I wore a diaper,
Every night and every day,

Now I use the potty so my pants stay clean and dry.
One day I can show Casey the way!

Each day I hop, I *jump*, I wait...

I slide, I paint, I run...

Casey sleeps and sleeps some more...

When will being a big brother be fun?

I don't like when Mommy says, "Be patient."
I don't like when Daddy says, "Please wait."

Why do babies need so *much* attention?
When will being a big brother be great?

Some days I have to be extra quiet,
when the baby takes a nap...

But some days when I sing and make silly faces...
I can even make Casey laugh and clap!

Splash! I help Mommy bathe the baby.

Sniff! I can bring
a new diaper, too.

March! I can help push Casey's stroller.
I'm starting to like the things a big brother can do!

Then one night I hear a sound...

Uh-oh! Casey's starting to cry!

I tiptoe out of bed...

Casey reaches for my finger...
And I sing my very own lullaby!

"I'm your big brother, Henry...
You're growing bigger every day...
There'll be so many things we can do together...
And that feels *great!* Hooray!"

Mom and Dad say Casey's lucky,
to have a big brother like me...
But want to know a secret?

I'm the one who's as
lucky as can be!